The Ice Dove
and
Other Stories

by

Diane de Anda

PIÑATA
BOOKS

Arte Público Press
Houston, Texas
1997

This volume is made possible through grants from the National Endowment for the Arts, Andrew W. Mellon Foundation, the Lila Wallace-Reader's Digest Fund and the City of Houston through the Houston Arts Alliance.

Piñata Books are full of surprises!

Piñata Books
An imprint of
Arte Público Press
University of Houston
4902 Gulf Fwy, Bldg 19, Rm 100
Houston, Texas 77204-2004

Text illustrations, cover illustration, and design by Bob Pharr

de Anda, Diane.
    The ice dove and other stories / by Diane de Anda.
        p.   cm.
    Summary: A collection of short stories in which Hispanic American children discover for themselves how special they are.
    ISBN 978-1-55885-189-4 (trade paper: alk. paper)
        1. Self-esteem—Juvenile fiction. 2. Hispanic Americans—Juvenile fiction. 3. Children's stories, American. [1. Self-esteem-Fiction. 2. Hispanic Americans—Fiction. 3. Short stories.]
    I. Title.
    PZ7.D3474Ic   1997
    [Fic]—dc21   96-50200
                                                          CIP
                                                          AC

♾ The paper used in this publication meets the requirements of the American National Standard for Permanence of Paper for Printed Library Materials Z39.48-1984.

Printed in the United States of America
May 2018–June 2018
Data Reproductions Corp., Auburn Hills, MI
11 10 9 8 7 6

The Ice Dove
and
Other Stories

The Ice Dove

Catalina lived with her grandfather in a white wood frame house with blue shutters. The house stood on the very top of a hill. From her window, she could see the fields that surrounded the house and the high buildings in the town down the road. Many years earlier, some of the fields were dotted with the livestock her grandfather raised, and others were planted in neat rows. Now her grandfather just boarded horses for some of the townspeople. He kept only chickens for himself, and in the warm seasons, he planted and tended to a small vegetable garden.

Two old dogs and a gray tabby lived in the barn. But Catalina's special pets lived on the window sill in her room. There sat her collection of forest animals her grandfather had carved for her from wood: cherry-colored squirrels, birch-gray deer, bears with stripes of wood grain down their rounded backs.

One very cold winter day, Catalina and *Abuelo*[1] climbed into his blue pickup truck and drove into the nearby town to buy some alfalfa bales for the horses. Snow stretched across the fields as far as they could see. As they traveled down the icy road, their breath came out in small clouds that stuck to the truck's windows.

When they got to town, *Abuelo* parked the truck in the space marked "loading zone." Catalina jumped out and carefully made her way on the icy sidewalk to Enrique's General Store. She entered the store and hurried to her favorite display in the big front window. There, on strings hanging from the ceiling, were a dozen, perfectly carved, crystal animals. When she touched them, the sunlight bounced rainbow colors about the room. Below were the larger animals, spread across a table like a glittering crystal zoo. In the middle of the covies of

[1] *Abuelo* means "grandfather" in Spanish.

birds sat a new piece Catalina had never seen before. It was a dove with graceful curves that formed its neck and rounded breast. Gently, she lifted it up and cupped it in her hands.

Her grandfather watched Catalina cradle the dove in her hands. He watched her eyes as she lifted the piece into the sunlight that filtered through the window. He felt sadness grow within him. He knew he could never buy the dove for her. Catalina knew it too and would never ask.

He paid for the bales that had already been loaded into the pickup truck. Then he walked up and put his hand on Catalina's shoulder.

"Come, Catalina, it's time to go," he said as he moved toward the door.

Catalina put the dove down carefully on the table. She put her hands in her pockets and backed out the front door, watching the dove as she left.

Abuelo drove home slowly on the icy road. When they drove up in front of the farmhouse, they noticed that icicles had

formed on the porch, hanging down from the roof in shiny silver slivers.

"See," remarked *Abuelo* as they walked up the stairs, "the icicles look like the crystals in the store, nature's crystals." *Abuelo* smiled as Catalina craned her neck and turned in a slow circle to view the icicles from every side.

Abuelo tugged on his gloves then reached up and snapped off an icicle. Catalina blinked, startled by the sharp pop it made. *Abuelo* took out his whittling knife and began to scrape the icicle. Puzzled, Catalina edged in closer to her grandfather and watched the curved figure of a dove appear through the crystal ice.

Soon *Abuelo* scraped the last chips of ice off the dove's pointed beak. Gently, *Abuelo* placed the ice dove in Catalina's hands. Catalina cradled the dove. Ignoring the prickly cold that stung her palms, she lifted the dove up to watch the sunlight spill through it. Catalina hugged her grandfather. *Abuelo* smiled, ruffled Catalina's hair, then went into the house.

"The dove is the most beautiful thing I have ever owned," she thought. "I want to keep it forever."

Catalina took the dove into her bedroom. She dumped the pennies out of the can she used for a bank and placed the dove inside the can. Bending down on her knees and elbows, she scooted the can under her bed. Then she sat back on her heels and smiled, content that her precious possession was safe.

Catalina walked into the kitchen and began helping *Abuelo* fix dinner. They cooked some white rice and a few carrots from the garden. They also warmed up some leftover chicken soup.

The broth felt soothing to their throats after breathing the icy air. *Abuelo* and Catalina talked about their trip into town. Catalina described the rainbow images that danced through the crystals in the store window.

"But my ice dove is the most beautiful of all," she insisted.

Abuelo just nodded and smiled.

After dinner, Catalina raced to her bedroom and reached under her bed for the can. She sat on the floor and stuck in her hand to pull out the ice dove. Her hand met icy water. Catalina's heart raced. She pulled the can to her face. Her ice dove was gone! All that remained was a lump of ice floating in the water.

Catalina felt her breath stick in her throat. Tears burned down her cheeks until the cries finally burst through. She lifted herself from the floor and ran with the can to her grandfather in the kitchen. She threw her arms around her grandfather.

Abuelo was stunned for a moment by Catalina's sudden entrance. He put his arms around her.

"*¿Qué pasó?* What's wrong?" he begged, cupping Catalina's face in his hands.

"My dove, my dove," she cried, and held the can toward her grandfather's face.

The old man gave a knowing sigh as he stroked Catalina's hair. "This was a wild dove. It needed to live outside. But, don't worry. We can set its spirit free."

Catalina stopped crying and gave her grandfather a puzzled look.

"Look," said *Abuelo* as he took the can from Catalina, placed it on the stove, and turned on the fire. Catalina walked up next to her grandfather and looked into the can.

"Now we must wait," *Abuelo* said as he put a lid over the can.

In a few minutes he beckoned to Catalina. "Watch, *m'ija*[2], the dove's spirit will rise out of the can and fly away to be free forever."

Abuelo lifted the lid. A small white cloud rose out of the can before Catalina's eyes. She watched as the mist moved and then slowly vanished into the air around her.

"It's free," *Abuelo* said as he put out his hand toward Catalina. "Come, I'll carve you another dove. But this one will have to live outside. We'll cut a hole in one of the snow drifts outside for the dove's house. You can visit it every day there until it flies away in the spring."

Catalina reached up and placed her hand in *Abuelo's*, and they walked out onto the front porch together.

---

[2]*M'ija* means "My daughter" in Spanish.

PINTO

Eight-year-old Ricky pressed his nose against the wire mesh on the rabbit hutch. He waited for his rabbit to look up and hop over to the door to greet him.

The brown-and-white spotted rabbit looked up quickly from his feeding dish as Ricky's shadow passed across him. Just as quickly, he scampered to the hutch door and listened for the familiar sound of the opening latch. He waited for the warmth of Ricky's arm reaching in to scratch his nose and let him out for his daily romp on the grass.

Ricky picked up his pet and cradled him in his arms. "Sorry, Pinto, no run on the grass right now. Today you're going to school with me. You're my science project!" Ricky said as he laughed and plopped the pudgy rabbit into his cardboard carrier.

꒰

Ricky had been waiting a long time to give his science presentation. The teachers always seemed to do things in alphabetical order, and with a name like Yanez-Ross, that meant he always had to be near the end, just before Alan Zimmerman. But that was okay, too, thought Ricky, because it had given him plenty of time to plan his project. It was going to be the best science project in the class!

He loaded Pinto's box into the back of the station wagon right next to the box full of all the equipment he had organized for his presentation. In the box were rabbit pellets, food and water dishes, books about rabbits, sketches and photos.

"You sure you have everything?" his mother called to him as she closed the front door and walked to the station wagon.

"Yeah, I checked and double-checked everything from my list when I packed the box last night," Ricky replied.

"You sound pretty organized to me," his mother remarked as she straightened the collar on his shirt. "This project's really important to you, isn't it?"

"It's going to be great, Mom!" Ricky flashed a broad smile and his mother smiled back at him in reply.

"Okay, let's hurry so we can put all this stuff in the classroom before the bell," said Ricky's mother as she closed and locked the station wagon's tailgate.

It was strange riding to school in the car on a sunny day. Since he lived only three blocks away, Ricky usually walked to school, except on rainy days. But this way he was going to be there thirty minutes early, so he could set everything up.

Ricky's mom pulled into the driveway right next to Ricky's classroom.

"Want help carrying your things in?" she asked.

"Thanks, Mom, but I can handle it from here by myself," Ricky replied quickly as he leapt from the car and dashed to the tailgate. It took three trips to the classroom and back again, but Ricky managed to lug Pinto and all his supplies into the classroom by himself.

"You managed that really well without any help, but does that mean that you're too big to give your mom a hug and a kiss good-bye?"

Ricky's mom looked at him, her dark eyes smiling. Ricky laughed, climbed across the car seat and gave his mom a quick kiss and a hug.

"I know you're going to do a terrific job on your report, *m'ijo*[3]," said Ricky's mother as she watched him slide from the seat onto the sidewalk and then shut the car door.

After he waved good-bye to his mom, Ricky began to feel more and more excited. He realized the day he had been looking forward to was finally here.

Inside the classroom, Ricky filled Pinto's food and water dishes and placed them in his carrier.

"You must be hungry and thirsty by now, old boy," he said, scratching Pinto behind the ears.

"What ya got there?"

Ricky turned to see Eddie and Mark trying to peer around him.

[3]*M'ijo* means "My son" in Spanish.

❧

"It's Pinto. I brought him for my science project today."

"Pinto," snapped Mark with a smirk on his face, "that's a horse's name. That sure is a funny-looking horse!"

Mark and Eddie began to laugh. Ricky's face began to feel hot. "Pinto just means spotted. See his white and brown spots?" he said, trying to ignore their laughing.

"Yeah, just like you, Ricky, half-white and half-brown," added Eddie.

Ricky took a deep breath and gritted his teeth. His hands made tight fists as he held them down at his sides, the hot feeling beginning to spread.

"Hey, Pinto," Mark called to Ricky as he and Eddie broke into backslapping laughter.

Ricky felt the hot tears welling up in his eyes. He took a breath and then bolted out the door. He ran so fast, the tears burning down his face, that before he realized it, he was standing on his porch.

He wasn't sure how long he stood catching his breath on the porch before his grandmother opened the door.

"Ricky, what are you doing here? I thought your mother dropped you off at school fifteen minutes ago."

He looked up at his grandmother. Then she saw his red, swollen eyes for the first time.

"Oh, *m'ijito*[4]," she called, walking over to him quickly and putting her arms around him. "Tell me what happened."

Ricky walked inside the house with her, sat hunched over on the couch and repeated the things Eddie and Mark had said.

"I could force you to go back, but you have to decide whether running away was the best way to handle this problem. You have to decide for yourself whether you're two halves or one whole person."

Ricky sat quietly on the couch for a few moments. He pictured Eddie and Mark pointing and laughing as he held Pinto in front of the class. Then he remembered all the afternoons he had spent at the library finding books on rabbits. He thought about

[4] *M'ijito* means "My little son" in Spanish.

❧

the evenings when he drew careful sketches on the kitchen table after dinner.

He hesitated, then slowly, but forcefully, sat up tall and straight on the couch. He wasn't exactly sure what his grandmother meant, but he knew no one was going to keep him from presenting his science project. He gave his grandmother a quick hug and dashed out the door to finish setting up his science project.

When he arrived at school, the room was filled with curious children milling around the rabbit carrier. As he approached, Mrs. Stewart, his teacher, motioned to all the children to go back to their seats and give Ricky room to prepare his presentation. As Mrs. Stewart took roll, Ricky practiced his speech in his mind. Finally, Mrs. Stewart called the class to face the table where Ricky stood alongside Pinto and his display.

Ricky began his speech as he had practiced for the past five days. He talked about the different parts of the rabbit's body, showing how the rabbit used its ears and feet. Pinto stomped his back foot on cue. He explained about the proper diet for rabbits and how to feed and care for them. He proudly passed around his collection of rabbit-care books.

Eddie raised his hand and asked, "How come he's all mixed up with brown and white splotches all over his back?"

Ricky took a slow, deep breath. "Actually, he's not mixed up at all," replied Ricky calmly. "He has beautiful brown and white markings that make him special and not like all the other rabbits.

"His parents were a beautiful brown and a beautiful white rex rabbit. Rex rabbits have special fur that feels like velvet and is thicker than other rabbits' fur because it grows in two layers. Pinto's mother was a white ermine rex. They have the thickest coat of all. He also got his mother's curly whiskers," Ricky added.

"Pinto's father was a Havana rex rabbit. It is also called a chocolate rex because its fur is thick and dark brown like a chocolate bar."

Some of the children smiled and licked their lips.

"Chocolate rex rabbits have special eyes. The color is brown, but look what happens in the dark."

Ricky nodded toward the teacher, and she quickly closed the window blinds. The room became shadowy.

"Look closely," Ricky told his classmates as he walked with Pinto around the room.

The children leaned forward and peered into Pinto's eyes. They glowed ruby red in the dim light.

When Ricky and Pinto returned to the table, the teacher flipped on the lights.

Ricky looked straight into Eddie's eyes. "I think he got the best of both! I call him Pinto because of his beautiful spotted fur."

Eddie turned his eyes away and began to fumble with an eraser on his desk.

Mrs. Stewart stood up and said, "Ricky, that was a wonderful presentation. I can tell you put a lot of hard work into preparing it."

She began to applaud and the class joined in. Eddie and Mark hesitated, then they applauded, too.

Ricky moved Pinto and his carrier onto a table in the back of the room. The rabbit inched its way toward Ricky.

"Thanks," he said as he rubbed his thumb gently across Pinto's nose.

Something Special

The seven a.m. sun tunneled its way into Luis Torres' bedroom through a small yellowed hole in the window shade. Luis wrinkled up his nose as the sunlight pressed against his face. He rolled on his side, still dreaming of riding in *abuelo's* red pickup truck.

Luis' mother walked quietly into the room past Luis' little brothers who were still sleeping. She leaned over the side of Luis' bed and gently moved her hand across the dark hair on his forehead. "Luis," she called softly, "time to get up. You have to get ready for school today, *m'ijo*."

Luis opened his eyes to see his mother's face smiling at him. Her dark hair fell forward and her gold-looped earrings shone in the morning light. Luis remembered it was

❧

Monday, the day he had to share something with the class.

"Okay, Mamá," said Luis as his mother bent down and kissed him on the forehead. His two little brothers snuggled closer together as his mother left the room. Luis put his feet on the cold floorboards. He looked at his turtle in the bowl next to his bed: "Good morning, Tortuga.[5] It's my turn at school today!"

Luis brushed his teeth slowly. In the mirror he imagined Eddie showing the class his new harmonica. Albert was showing the class pictures of the animals he saw at the San Diego Zoo.

Luis stopped brushing his teeth. The toothpaste foam rolled down the side of his mouth. He began to practice his speech in his mind: "I am Luis Torres. I want to show you . . . to show you what?" What could he show the class? He couldn't bring Tortuga. Mike Stevens had brought his turtle last week. Besides, he wanted to show them something special, something about Luis Torres.

---

[5]Tortuga means "turtle" in Spanish.

❧

"Who told you that was the way to brush your teeth? Boy, are you a mess!" his sister Lucy remarked, looking over his shoulder.

Luis looked in the mirror and saw the toothpaste foam driveling over his chin. He lifted his toothbrush to flick the white foam onto his sister. Lucy screamed and dashed out the door. "How could she bug me about toothpaste on a day like this!" he thought as he washed away the foam and stepped into the warm bath water. "Hey, *niño*[6], what's taking you so long? Breakfast is waiting for you on the table," said Luis' father as he passed through the hall.

"Papá, I need something for school today," Luis called from the bathtub.

"Okay, what is it you need, *m'ijo*?" his father said as he stepped into the room.

"I have to share something with the class today, but I don't have anything to share," Luis replied as he looked up at his father.

"Sure you do. How about *Tortuga*?"

Luis shook his head.

---

[6]*Niño* means "child" in Spanish.

❧

His father continued, "Hmmm. How about your football or one of your books?"

Luis shook his head again.

"Anybody can bring that. I want to show something that is only mine."

"Well, I guess then you'll have to think about it and decide what is special to you," his father said as he left the bathroom.

Luis pressed his lips together and wrinkled his forehead as he thought. He knew his father was right; only he knew what was right for Luis Torres.

Lucy, Mamá, Papá, and *Abuelo* (Luis' grandfather) were already at the table. Papá and *Abuelo* were warming their hands with their coffee cups. Mamá was pouring hot chocolate into Luis' cup.

She called to Luis, "Come on, *m'ijo*, your chorizo and eggs are getting cold."

Luis walked over to the table and sat down next to Lucy, who was busy eating her breakfast. Papá and *Abuelo* were talking about the repairs needed on the pickup truck.

❦

Luis put a piece of egg into his mouth. He sat motionless, going over all his possessions in his mind.

"You think it's going to melt in your mouth or something?" said Lucy, breaking Luis out of his daydream.

"Huh?" he answered, quickly shoveling more eggs into his mouth.

"Boy, you're really out of it today. What's your problem?" Lucy leaned toward her brother.

"I have to share today in class, and I don't know what to take."

"How about *Tortuga* or your baseball mitt?" Lucy offered.

"Anybody can bring an old baseball mitt. It's got to be something that says, 'this is me, Luis Torres!'"

Lucy shrugged her shoulders and wiped a chocolate moustache from her face.

Papá and *Abuelo* stopped talking and looked at Luis. Papá leaned toward the tall, white-haired old man and whispered something in his ear.

❧

Abuelo stood and pressed Luis' shoulder softly. "Come with me," he called, and walked toward his room.

Luis followed *Abuelo*, catching the sharp smell of shaving soap as he entered the bedroom. *Abuelo* leaned over his large cherry-colored cedar chest. His hands passed smoothly through years of memories. At last he sighed softly. "Here it is," he said, and turned toward Luis. *Abuelo* pulled out a box of animals made of tin.

"Why are you taking out the Christmas tree ornaments, *Abuelo*?" asked Luis.

"Because here is something special you did that you can be proud of."

Abuelo took out a set of five tin animal ornaments: a horse, a sheep, a reindeer and two doves. "Remember, *mi'jito*, how I taught you to make them, the way my father taught me, and his before that?"

Luis held two of the ornaments up to the light: the brown reindeer with the yellow antlers and a pudgy white and silver sheep.

"They're special because you made them yourself with your own hands. No one else will have anything like this, nobody," said *Abuelo,* handing him the rest of the animals.

"That's the trouble," thought Luis, "no one else would probably do something like this."

He looked down at the animals. Then he remembered how much he had enjoyed working with *Abuelo* to make each tin form come alive in shape and color.

His grandfather saw his hesitation, ruffled Luis' hair, and said, "It's up to you, *m'ijo,*" and left the room.

Luis walked back slowly to his bedroom and laid the pieces on his desk. A crystal unicorn he had won pitching balls at a carnival caught his eye as the sun threw flecks of silver light across it. His eyes moved back and forth from the crystal figure to the tin ornaments. Finally, he scooped up the ornaments and the crystal figure with one swoop and eased them into his backpack. Just then he heard his mother call. It was time to leave. Luis slipped his backpack on his back and ran out to the car.

"Well, *m'ijo*," his mother asked, "have you decided what you're sharing with the class today?"

"Yeah, have you?" his sister repeated.

"Sort of, " he replied, carefully easing the backpack onto the car seat. All the way to school his mind kept shifting between the images of the crystal and the tin ornaments. As they arrived at the school gate, Luis felt the images begin to blur.

"Wake up, sleepyhead," his sister called as she jumped out of the car. Luis kissed his mother good-bye, then slowly moved toward the classroom, the images spinning in his head.

Luis felt a slight pang in his stomach as he took his seat. He sat quietly through roll call, waiting for his time to share.

The teacher finally called, "Luis, it's your turn to share today."

Luis smiled, unzipped his backpack and reached in to get his objects to share with the class.

He stepped to the front of the class and held up the crystal unicorn. "See this?" he began. "It is an animal someone carved out of crystal glass. It must have been hard work to make a piece of glass look like this." He held the unicorn up high to catch the reflected light.

"My Grampa and I make animals, too," he continued. "Our whole family has for years, out of tin." Luis held up the ornaments. "I made these myself. My abuelo showed me the special way his father taught him to cut them out and put on color."

"A week before Christmas, my brothers and sister and all my cousins meet at my Grampa's workshop in the garage. We all draw pictures on metal strips: stars and candles and wreaths, but mostly animals. *Abuelo* helps us cut out the shapes with his big metal snipers. Then we put on the special paints and glazes that make the ornaments shine."

"On Christmas Eve everyone comes to our house for a big party. My uncles bring out their guitars and we all sing. There's lots of food, like turkey and tamales and a great big piñata filled with candy and toys."

Luis closed his eyes for a second. A spinning piñata danced before his eyes, a blur of red, white, and green.

He smiled and continued. "At sunset we all gather around the Christmas tree and take turns putting our ornaments on the tree. My Grampa and all the grownups put on the ornaments they made when they were children, and all the grandchildren put on their shiny new ones."

"Finally, *Abuelo* puts the huge tin angel his father made almost one hundred years ago on the top of the tree. Then we turn on the lights, and all the ornaments shine a beautiful silver and red and blue and gold."

Luis held the ornaments up higher. The silver metal and the bright coatings threw rays of color across the room. A sigh swept in a ripple across the class.

Luis smiled and took his seat again. He placed the objects on his desk. He watched the bright patterns of light spill across his desk as the sunlight passed through the crystal unicorn and bounced off the tin ornaments. Luis cupped his hands on the top of his desk to catch the glimmering sunlight. He smiled as the sunlight danced on his palms.

❧

THE CHRISTMAS
SPIRIT TREE

Friday afternoon trilled with the high-pitched sounds of children rushing out of Ninth Avenue Elementary School into the beginning of Christmas vacation. Children stood in wiggling rows, weaving into their big yellow buses with shiny red and green Christmas projects tucked under their arms and into backpacks empty of their usual books and binders.

Marika, Tonia and Roberto snaked their way together through the lines of buzzing, ever-moving children to the street corner. There Mrs. Sánchez, the crossing guard, greeted them with a smile. As she nodded her head toward them, the bell on the top of the Santa's hat she wore that day gave a cheery ring.

"Buenas tardes, niños.[7] And what are all those pretty things you're carrying?" she called to them. Marika, the youngest of the three, pressed forward with her shiny red foil ball. She stood on tiptoe and held it up for Mrs. Sánchez to see. "It's for our tree. I'm going to put it up real high so the sun will make it shine," the excited seven-year-old said in rapid-fire speed.

"Yes, it's beautiful, Marika. I always look for your Christmas tree each year when I drive down the street."

Marika, Tonia and Roberto responded with a chorus of smiles. Their Christmas tree, a family tradition that they were proud of, had now become an annual event for the neighborhood as well. A twelve-foot-tall pine with branches that swung out in perfect, even, deep green arcs stood in the middle of their front yard. On the Saturday before Christmas, their father took the big carton full of Christmas bulbs and lights

---

[7]*Buenas tardes, niños,* means "good afternoon children" in Spanish.

and glittering gold garlands out of the garage. Papá would make the strings of bulbs flow in beautiful rings of light around the tree.

Then it was their turn. Mamá would balance delicately on the ladder as the children handed her the green and gold and red bulbs and pointed to the branch where they wanted her to place them. Sometimes Papá would lift them up or let them sit on his shoulders to put some of the decorations high on the tree.

But mostly, the bottom half of the tree was theirs. They packed the bottom half with bulbs, foil balls, decorated pie tins and other decorations they made until it burst with color. Then everyone would step back as Papá threw the switch. Suddenly there was a rush of color as the tree lights went on to the cheers of the three children.

The three Pérez children crossed the street, waved good-bye to Mrs. Sánchez, and continued down the half block to their house. Marika couldn't keep the slow, steady pace of her brother and sister. She was too excited to walk in an everyday way. She sailed ahead in a long leaping skip, her shoulder-length dark hair bouncing about her face and head. Marika didn't stop until she reached the tree. She dropped her backpack onto the grass and walked up to the tree with the red foil ball in her hand. Marika stood on her tiptoes and leaned up into the tree. She held onto a heavy lower branch to balance herself as she hooked her red foil ball as far above her head as she could reach. She fell back onto her flat feet and tilted her head to watch the sunlight play on the ornament's shiny surface.

"Hey, it's not time to decorate yet," Roberto insisted as he entered the yard.

"I know, I know," replied Marika. "I'm just practicing. Papá will help me put it higher tomorrow."

Eleven-year-old Roberto might have argued with Marika last year, but he was a sixth-grader now and was not about to argue with a second-grader over a big wad of aluminum foil. He just shook his head and walked in the front door.

❧

Marika reached out and grasped two green sprigs on a lower branch. One in each hand, she rocked back and forth singing, *"Feliz Navidad, Feliz Navidad*[8] . . . I want to wish you a Merry Christmas. I want to wish you a Merry Christmas."* She hummed the melody as the song Mamá played on her stereo trailed out of her memory.

When Tonia passed by, Marika called out, "Come on, Tonia, come and dance with me. There's plenty of room."

Tonia laughed. "This is crazy," she replied as Marika reached out to pull her into the celebration. The two girls locked fingers then leapt on tiptoe around the tree, laughing together at their silliness as they danced their way into Christmas vacation.

On their second trip around the tree, they spotted their father coming through the gate. The girls broke their rhythm and dashed to the gate to meet him. Before he could greet them, they grabbed onto the sleeves of his jacket, jumping up and down, asking when they could decorate the tree.

[8]*Feliz Navidad,* means "Merry Christmas" in Spanish.

❦

Mr. Pérez smiled. This playful pleading was part of their family tradition. They would beg and wheedle for the decorations a day early, but he would remind them that Saturday morning was the traditional decorating day. By the time they reached the porch, the girls had accepted that the decorating would have to wait until tomorrow.

≈ ≈ ≈

That evening Tonia and Marika rushed through dinner so they could prepare for the following morning. They set the table at top speed. When dinner was served, they scooped heaping spoonfuls of food into their mouths so they could excuse themselves and dash to the work table in their bedroom.

In the bedroom, Tonia pulled out a cardboard box filled with paints and other art supplies: pieces of colored paper, cellophane and red, green and gold foil. As soon as she placed the box on the table, their fingers played through the contents, plucking out the pieces that sparked ideas for new ornaments for the tree. Tonia carefully traced

≈

the outline of a bell across a piece of heavy gold foil. Marika admired how easily Tonia outlined and cut its perfect shape. Tonia smiled at Marika's admiring glance. "Come on. I'll help you cut out your decorations," Tonia encouraged and leaned across to cut round and diamond and oblong shapes into the sheets of foil Marika had spread across the table.

When their mother knocked on the door at nine o'clock to say good night, Marika and Tonia had a table filled with foil ornaments. Each one was painted in bright colors with a different design.

"They're wonderful!" Mamá exclaimed as she looked at the glimmering lines of color across the table.

Marika and Tonia were happy it was bedtime. They quickly changed, brushed their teeth, exchanged family good night wishes and hugs and leapt into bed. They knew the sooner they slept, the sooner tomorrow would come.

The morning sunlight stole into the girls' bedroom, tickling them across their eyelashes to wake up. Marika blinked, opened her eyes briefly, then closed her eyes and started to pull the blankets over her head to block out the morning sun and lull herself back to sleep. But then she remembered: It was Saturday. It was time to decorate the tree. She bolted into a sitting position and gave a great yawning stretch. Then she shook her sister.

"Wake up, Tonia. Wake up. It's morning. Come on, let's get our box of decorations and start now."

Tonia made soft grumbling sounds at Marika and buried her face in her pillow.

"Okay, okay," responded Marika. "I'll do it myself."

She bounded from the bed and walked over to pick up the box of decorations they had made last night. With careful steps, delicately balancing the awkward, bulky box, she moved down the hall toward the front door. In the still and quiet morning, she could hear every footstep down the long hallway as she passed the other family members enjoying their Saturday morning rest. Marika parted with her precious box for only a moment when she placed it on a table to free her hands to unlock and open the front door.

She balanced the box down the front steps, blinking at the bright sunlight that poured over her. At the bottom of the steps, she began to take larger, more bounding steps as her eagerness to begin the decorating grew.

She had taken only three steps when she came to an abrupt halt. Marika stood frozen, her mouth wide open. For a minute she remained motionless, staring in disbelief. There, where the tree had always been, was a stump, broken and jagged, with a few small branches and pine needles scattered around it. Suddenly she broke free from her trance. Without thinking, she let the box drop from her arms and ran yelling into the house.

"Mamá, Papá, help, help, it's gone, it's gone." She kept repeating this as she tore into the house and down the hallway to her parents' bedroom and leapt onto their bed.

Her startled parents sat up, confused and anxious, seeing Marika shouting at the foot of their bed.

Suddenly, Marika began to cry. She covered her face, shouting between sobs, "It's gone, It's gone."

By this time, her parents were very concerned. Her mother quickly moved toward the foot of the bed, took Marika into her arms and gently rocked her and stroked her hair. Her father got out of bed and came over to the edge of the bed.

"*¿Qué pasó m'ija?* What happened, Marika? Why are you so upset?" he asked.

Marika held her breath a moment and clenched her jaw to stop her crying. Between sobs she blurted out, "The tree is gone. Somebody took the tree. It's gone!"

"You must have had a bad dream," her father replied, gently wiping the streaks of tears from her cheeks.

"No, no, it's really true. Come, come with me and see."

Marika leapt from her mother's arms and beckoned her parents to follow her. By this time the noise had also awakened Roberto

and Tonia, so all four followed Marika down the hallway and out the front door. Mamá gasped; Tonia sighed, "No," and buried her teary face in her mother's robe. Papá yelled, "*Dios Mío*, My God," and walked up to the stump with a dazed Roberto close behind. Roberto felt the tears well in his eyes as he looked at the maimed and broken stump.

"Who could have done this, Papá? Why?" Roberto pleaded.

"Who can understand why someone would do such a thing?" Papá replied.

"How could someone steal a Christmas tree? How could someone celebrate Christmas around a stolen tree?" Mamá added.

"They probably took it to sell it," replied Papá. "Let's see if they left a trail."

Papá followed lines of fallen needles and a few small pieces of branch across the lawn and sidewalk to the curb.

"Looks like they loaded it into a car or truck here," he said at the end of the trail. He looked down into the street. There alongside the curb was the red foil ball Marika had left on the tree the day before. He picked it up and shook off some dust, then slowly walked over to Marika with it.

"Here, *m'ija*," he said, putting it into her hands. "At least we have your beautiful decoration."

Marika pressed her lips into as much of a smile as she could manage.

Tonia finally moved forward and surveyed the empty lawn.

"What are we going to do, Papá?" she asked.

"I'm not sure yet, but I think it's important that we don't let the person who stole the tree also steal our Christmas spirit away. Let's get on with our day and discuss it at dinner time."

"And let's start with a good breakfast," Mamá added. "Remember, we're going to the mall to see Santa today."

The three children managed weak smiles and huddled around their mother as they all went in to eat and get ready to finish their Christmas shopping.

Papá stayed out surveying the yard. Then he walked up and down the block, talking to the neighbors about what had happened. He hoped to find some leads or some explanation, but no one had seen or heard anything. Dogs had barked a few times during the night, but they always barked at cats or strays and no one ever paid much attention. Everyone was not only shocked and sad for the Pérez family, but felt they had lost an important part of their own Christmas as well.

≈ ≈ ≈

Tonia, Roberto and Marika looked different from the other children in the line to talk to Santa. The other children talked in quick, excited voices to each other or their parents. The three Pérez children stood silently looking at the floor or sightlessly ahead. They had all written and practiced their lists. They knew exactly what they were going to say. But now, they didn't feel the same anticipation of good things to come that they had other years. Tonia and Roberto gave polite smiles, recited their lists, took their candy canes and scooted off the stage.

≈

A wry smile came over Marika as she approached Santa. Unable to contain herself, she ran up to Santa, grabbed his sleeve and blurted out, "You can get it back for us, Santa, can't you? Please bring back our tree for Christmas."

Santa gave a puzzled look towards Mrs. Pérez, who stood behind Marika.

"I'm sorry, Santa. Marika doesn't understand. Someone cut down and stole the Christmas tree that has been growing in front of our house for as long as we've lived there. That's the tree she wants back."

Santa's face looked sad and serious as he turned toward Marika. "I'll see what I can do to help, but even Santa can't make things just like they were before. But I promise you something special will happen this Christmas that will make you feel happy again."

Marika said thank you with a broad and hopeful smile as she took her mother's hand and walked off stage. She ran up to Tonia and Roberto and declared, "Santa said we're going to get our tree back."

"That's not exactly what he said," her mother interrupted.

❧

"I know," she continued, "but he promised to make everything okay—right, Mamá?"

"Well, I guess he did. We'll just have to believe and wait and see," replied Mrs. Pérez with a worried look on her face.

"No one can fix a cut-up tree," added Roberto, trying to sound very logical and grown-up.

"You'll see," said Marika. "You'll see."

≫ ≫ ≫

When they arrived home, their father met them at the door with a big smile on his face.

"Hurry up, come on in. I've got a surprise for all of you."

The children and Mrs. Pérez rushed in the door and dropped their packages, bundles and bags onto the couch and coffee table. There in the middle of the front room was a six-foot-tall Christmas tree, balanced delicately on a wooden stand.

"I know each year we have a little tree inside the house, because our big tree is out-

≫

side, so I thought this year we'd just decorate a bigger tree inside the house." Mr. Pérez scanned his children's faces. They looked at the tree. It was a pretty green. It's branches were nice and even, and it had that wonderful pine smell. But it wasn't their tree, their family tree.

"It's a real nice tree," began Tonia.

"Yeah, Dad, thanks," added Roberto.

"This isn't the surprise Santa promised," thought Marika. "I know it isn't."

"We'll decorate it tomorrow on Christmas Eve like we do every year," interjected Mamá. "Thanks, honey, for finding such a nice tree. Now, let's wash up for dinner, so we can begin wrapping all these presents."

Dinner was quiet that evening. Mrs. Pérez described the gifts she had found for the grandparents. The children listened and poked at the food on their plates.

"Come on, finish your dinner. You always have a good time helping me wrap the presents," Mamá insisted.

After the dishes were cleared, the children all got into their traditional Christmas-wrapping roles. Tonia was the expert bow-maker. Her slender fingers twisted and darted, transforming flat strips of ribbon into beautiful curving loops that sat atop the presents like clusters of red and green butterflies. Roberto was the packager. He transformed the flattened gift boxes into square and rectangular containers. His keen sense of space knew exactly the right size for each item. He could always tell the exact length he needed to cut the shiny foil or candy-cane-printed wrapping paper. Mamá and Papá twisted the paper expertly around all the sides and corners of the gift boxes, but it was Marika who was always there as needed to attach the pieces of Scotch tape that kept everything in place.

Mamá put on tapes of Christmas carols to help get everyone in a holiday mood. Everyone listened as they worked, but somehow no one sang along as they had other years.

❧

By nine-thirty, towers of bright and shiny wrapped presents surrounded the Pérez family.

"Great job!" said Mamá, picking up the last scraps of wrapping paper.

"Yes, I'm impressed by how well you all did. Maybe I'll hire you out next year," added Papá with a wink toward Mamá.

Mamá moved toward each child and gave them a hug and kiss on the head. "Hurry on to bed now. Tomorrow's a big day. We still have a tree to decorate."

The children stole a quick look at the tree in the corner of the room, then said good night and headed down the hall toward their rooms.

"It is a nice tree, I guess," said Tonia.

Roberto just shrugged.

≈ ≈ ≈

The next morning, the girls stirred in their beds as sounds of "O Christmas Tree" filtered into their room. They incorporated the sounds into their Christmas dreams until Roberto burst into their room.

≈

"Tonia, Marika, get up, get up. Some people are here singing outside our door."

As the girls sat up, they saw their parents moving down the hall in their robes, their mother saying, "Who ever heard of Christmas caroling in the morning? Who do you think it could be?"

"There's only one way to find out," Papá replied, moving a little faster down the hall.

The girls leapt out of bed, and the three children ran to catch up with their parents.

As they entered the front room, the singing became louder.

Papá stepped ahead and opened the door. There assembled in a semi-circle in their front yard were about fifteen of their friends and neighbors, singing in loud smiling voices.

In the middle of the group in a large planter box was a beautiful eight-foot-tall pine tree, with long, full limbs reaching out in perfect symmetrical arcs.

Mrs. Sánchez stepped forward, the bell on her Santa hat jingling as she walked.

"We know it isn't the same as your own tree, and it's not quite as big yet, but if we plant it now, we can all watch it grow together."

Mr. Pérez bit down hard to hold back the feelings that welded up in his chest and throat. He hesitated a minute, trying to find words that could express all the feelings of joy and gratitude he felt at that moment. He began, "What can I say to such generous friends?"

Before he could finish, Marika ran forward into the middle of the group.

"I know," she cried. "I know what to say. Thank you for delivering the tree Santa promised me."

Soft laughter rose from the group. Then the friends and neighbors pressed forward, sharing hugs and shaking hands. The women dabbed their eyes, and some of the men rolled the huge planter box to a place near the old tree's stump. Together they began to break the earth with the picks and shovels they had brought along. Before long, the new tree stood securely in place, its graceful green branches reaching out towards the crowd.

Marika ran into the house, scooped up her red foil ball and returned quietly to the tree. Mamá nudged Papá to look at Marika. He walked over and in one easy movement had her sitting high on his shoulders.

Marika reached up and with swift and careful fingers hooked the ball onto the highest branch.

The crowd clapped and cheered spontaneously. Marika smiled at the brilliant sunlight dancing on her foil ball and the warm and happy glow that it lit within her.